First edition 2018
Library of Congress Control Number: 2017956677
ISBN 978-1-60991-208-6 (USA)
ISBN 978-1-78475-966-7 (UK)

10 9 8 7 6 5 4 3 2 1

Printed in China

This book was typeset in Athelas.
The illustrations were created traditionally
and in mixed media.
Book design by Rose Audette

Ripley Entertainment Inc.
7576 Kingspointe Parkway, Suite 188
Orlando, Florida 32819
Email: publishing@ripleys.com
visit us at www.ripleys.com/books

Young Arrow
20 Vauxhall Bridge Road
London SW1V 2SA

Young Arrow is part of the Penguin Random House
group of companies whose addresses can be found at
global.penguinrandomhouse.com.

Penguin
Random House
UK

First published in Great Britain in 2018
by Young Arrow

www.penguin.co.uk

A CIP catalogue record for
this book is available from
the British Library.

SHARKEE

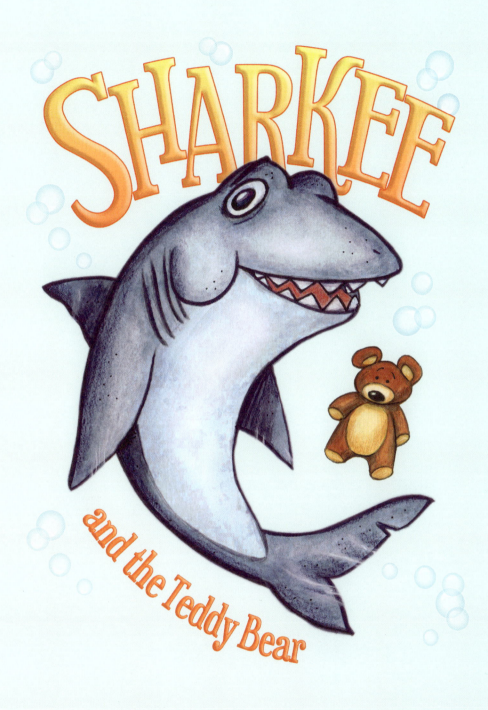

and the Teddy Bear

Carrie Bolin and Jessica Firpi

Illustrated by John Graziano

RIPLEY

PUBLISHING

a Jim Pattison Company

Hey, what's that?

It looks like a teddy bear!

But, sharks don't need teddy bears...

Where did it go?

We decided to look for it.

We asked the blue lobster.

He wasn't very helpful.

The urchin, well, he didn't see anything.

The stingray wouldn't say.

The octopus was a little startled.

We didn't stay to chat.

And the boxer crab?

We didn't stand a fighting chance.

What if I *never* find the teddy bear?